A LITTLE LONGER

First published in 2018 in Great Britain by
Barrington Stoke Ltd
18 Walker Street, Edinburgh, EH3 7LP

www.barringtonstoke.co.uk

Text © 2018 Bali Rai

A CIP catalogue record for this book is available
from the British Library upon request

ISBN: 978-1-78112-832-9

Printed in China by Leo

STAY A LITTLE LONGER

BALI RAI

Barrington Stoke

PROLOGUE

I wrote Dad a letter before he died. It was the second letter I had ever written. The first was to Santa Claus, written in purple felt-tip pen and addressed to Lapland. I was six years old.

I wrote my second letter – the one to Dad – when I was twelve. He had been ill for a year. At first, he seemed OK. Sometimes his treatment made him sick, but nothing too bad. Then he got worse. I remember an ambulance taking him away. After that, he stayed in hospital. He lost so much weight that his bones stuck out, and he went bald.

Dad cried and told me he was sorry all the time. But I knew it wasn't his fault.

"Don't be sorry," I told him. "You'll feel much better soon."

But I knew that wasn't true either.

After one of the hospital visits, Mum sat me down and tried to explain what was happening. I just nodded. Mum tried to say the right things. Tried to stay calm. But I didn't want her to. I *wanted* Mum to be sad, because that was honest. I hate it when people try to protect me from things. And I was sad too – I still am. No, that's wrong. I was *more* than sad. I felt hollow inside. The world around me kept on going, and I felt like an outsider. I couldn't think straight. I couldn't even taste my food.

Dad never saw my letter. He died before I found the courage to show him. That was over a year ago now, but I still have the letter. It isn't very long. It doesn't say anything amazing or clever. It's just my thoughts, put into words.

I didn't want Dad to leave us, to leave me. I didn't want him to be in so much pain. I wanted him to stay. I wanted him to be the Dad he was before things went wrong. I just wanted him to stay a little longer ...

"*What?*" the tall lad asked me. "Who calls their dog Milly? Typical girl!"

The lad was smiling but not in a good way. Around his wide mouth he had a small beard, which hung off his chin. His smile reminded me of a goat. I looked up and down the path, hoping to see an adult. But the cold, sunny park was oddly empty for a Saturday afternoon. Normally I liked that, but not today.

"My dog would batter yours," his mate added. He was small and spotty, with too much gel in his hair. He got his phone out and started to film us.

"YouTube, innit!" his friend said.

The lads were Asian, like me. They both wore caps and black puffa jackets, with skinny jeans and trainers. Like it was a uniform or something.

"Just go away!" I said as I wondered why they were picking on me.

They didn't listen. The tall lad kicked out at Milly. She whimpered and hid behind my legs. She was just a puppy – my new pet.

"Leave Milly alone!" I yelled.

"Stupid dog, shit name," the tall lad said.

I started to walk away, but he grabbed at Milly's purple lead.

"*GERROFF!*" I screamed.

"Make me!" he said, and shoved me aside.

I started to cry, and he just laughed at me.

"*What are you doing?!*" I heard someone shout.

An older man stormed towards us. I recognised him – he'd just moved into a house on the same street as me and Mum. But I'd never spoken to him before. He was short and stocky, and looked angry. I was relieved to see him.

"Run!" the tall boy said as he let go of Milly's leash. "Run before Granddad bites us with his false teeth!"

The older man stood between the boys and me.

"What's wrong with you?" he asked. "Why would you pick on a child?"

The tall boy swore.

"You want some licks, bruv?" he asked as he clenched his fists.

The old man shook his head. His arms were thick with muscle, and his hands were huge.

"Don't make me laugh," he said. "Be on your way, son, before I do something I regret."

The smaller boy spoke up.

"You can't touch us!" he said. "Got you on camera, innit?"

The man turned, and I got a closer look at him. He had short grey hair and a scar across his left cheek. His eyes were pale brown with flecks of green.

"Ignore these idiots," he said to me. "Are you OK?"

"I think so," I said.

The lads seemed annoyed at being ignored. The tall one swore a few more times, but the man didn't respond. Soon they grew bored and left.

"Shall I call the police?" the old man asked.

"I'll just go home," I told the man. "I only live up the road."

"I know," he said. "I've seen you around. I can call your dad, if you like?"

I shook my head.

"No," I said. "I ... er ..."

"All right," the man replied. "But I'll walk with you, just in case ..."

I knew to be careful about strangers, but the man wasn't one. He was a neighbour and seemed kind. I thought about something Dad had taught me. Most people are decent, he'd said. You just have to give them a chance. I smiled at my neighbour and nodded.

"I think that would be OK," I told him. "I'm Aman."

"Pleased to meet you, Aman," he said. "I'm Gurnam Singh. Your name is Punjabi, like mine."

I shrugged but didn't reply. Gurnam knelt down to pet Milly. She was wary of him for a moment but soon relaxed. Milly nibbled at his fingers and wagged her tail.

"I always wanted a Golden Retriever," Gurnam told me. "From those toilet roll adverts ..."

"Milly's a Labrador Retriever," I explained, and hoped that I didn't sound rude. "That's the dog from the adverts. But people often get the two breeds confused."

"Really?" Gurnam asked. "I never knew that."

"Did you love those adverts when you were young, too?" Those adverts were my favourites. It was why I chose Milly.

"Ha ha – yeah," Gurnam replied. "But that was a long time ago."

When we got home and Mum opened the door, she looked shocked.

"Er ... *hello*," Mum said as Milly bounced past her legs, yapping away.

"Hi, Mum," I said. "This is Gurnam – he lives a few doors away."

"Yes," Mum said. "I've seen him around. But what's going on ...?"

"Some older boys were being mean to Milly," I explained. "Gurnam helped me."

Mum's expression grew stern.

"What boys?" she asked. "Did you get their names?"

"Just some idiots," Gurnam told her. "I hope you don't mind that I walked Aman home."

"Not at all," Mum said. "Thank you. It's very kind of you."

"I would have called you or your husband, but Aman seemed fine," Gurnam added.

Mum smiled sadly and replied, "It's just me and Aman. Her dad ... he isn't *around* any more."

Gurnam nodded.

"Well," he said. "Better be off. Pleasure to meet you both."

"We should thank you properly," Mum said. "Why don't you come for tea one evening?"

Gurnam smiled. "That would be lovely."

I watched as he walked away.

"What a nice man," Mum said.

"Yeah," I said. "Can I have McDonald's for tea? *Please ...?*"

Mum shook her head.

"The amount of chicken nuggets you eat, you'll turn *into* one," she said. "You can have risotto and salad with me."

I glanced out at Gurnam before shutting the door. He stopped and turned. But now he wasn't smiling. He just looked sad.

2

At school, I told Lola about the boys who'd attacked Milly.

"That's *so* wrong," Lola replied.

Lola was my best friend. But to be honest, she was my *only* friend. I had known Lola since we'd been babies. I had other friends at primary school, but I stopped talking to them when Dad got sick. After Dad went, I didn't talk at all for a while, and Lola was the only friend who stuck around. Lola's nan, Olivia, lived next door. She was like my nan, too.

"Why would they want to harm such a cute thing as Milly?" Lola added. "Stupid dumbasses!"

Mrs Cooper heard her and said, "Lola!"

"Sorry, miss," Lola said.

She'd tied up her straight dark hair in a ponytail and her pale-brown eyes shone behind her black glasses. Lola's eye shape came from her dad, whose family were Chinese. But her parents were divorced, so she only saw her dad once a month.

"Do you know their names?" Lola whispered to me.

"No," I replied. "They're just local lads. I've seen them before. Anyway, it doesn't matter now."

"But what if they do it again?" Lola said.

I had been worried about that since Saturday night. I'd had bad dreams about it. But I didn't tell Mum. She'd had enough stress lately.

Mrs Cooper called me over and said, "Mrs West says you're helping with our Community Garden project, Aman?"

I nodded.

"I didn't know you were a gardener," Mrs Cooper added.

"Mrs West said it would be good for me," I said, being honest

My form tutor smiled and told me, "I'm sure it will. It's useful to have a hobby."

"Dad used to garden," I said. I remembered how he'd walk into the house with muddy boots on and Mum would tell him off. And he'd wink at me and pull a face to make me giggle.

"Runs in the family, then," Mrs Cooper replied.

"Guess so, miss," I said.

When I got home, Milly barked with delight. She scampered towards me and slipped onto her behind.

"Hey, you!" I said, giving her a cuddle.

Milly nuzzled against me. I sniffed her head, the way Dad used to sniff mine when I was small. We'd watch *Ben & Holly* together, and I'd rub my head on Dad's stubbly chin.

"You smell," I told Milly. "Like, *bad* ..."

I went up to my room and started my homework. Milly jumped onto my bed and lay down, her tail wagging.

"I'll play with you later," I told her.

But I couldn't focus. After Dad went, it was like a dark cloud of depression followed me around. These days it was more grey than black, but it still weighed me down sometimes. I moved to my bed, held on to Milly and tried to switch off my dark thoughts.

"I suppose I should walk you," I said after a while.

Only I didn't want to. I wanted to shut out the whole world. I pulled Milly even closer, and she began to lick my face.

"Come on, then!" I sighed.

I stayed alert as we walked, just in case those boys turned up. I wasn't really scared, just wary. After a while, I walked back by the park, without going in. It was getting colder, and I still had my school uniform on. Tiny flecks of rain tickled my face.

Then Milly began to pull on her lead.

"What's the matter?" I asked her.

She started yapping at something on the other side of the park railings.

"Have you seen a squirrel?" I said.

Milly began to pull harder.

"Milly!" I shouted.

And then I spotted Gurnam. He was sitting on his own on a bench inside the park. Milly ran over and yapped with delight. I followed her through the gate.

"Hi," I said.

Gurnam nodded. He hadn't shaved and seemed worn out. His eyes looked sore, as if he'd been crying or something.

"Hello again," Gurnam replied in a dull voice. He petted Milly but didn't seem very interested in her – or me.

"Thanks for the other day," I said. "It was really kind of you."

"No problem," Gurnam replied as Milly padded back to me.

He looked sad again, and I began to wonder why.

"Are you OK?" I asked without thinking. After all, it was none of my business.

"I don't know," he told me. "Sometimes I just ..."

Gurnam stopped and shook his head.

"Don't worry about me," he replied. "I'm just a silly old man."

"Well, if you ever ..." I began, but I didn't know what I wanted to say. The words just died in my throat.

"If I ever what ...?" Gurnam asked.

"Doesn't matter," I said. "It was lovely to see you."

"You too," he replied.

I started to walk away, but something made me stop. I remembered Dad telling me about kindness. He'd said it doesn't cost a thing. And sometimes life isn't easy. If we can help others along the way, we should. I turned back to Gurnam.

"We're having pasta for tea," I told him. "Do you want to come over?"

I waited for Gurnam to say no, but he didn't. Instead, he stood up and wiped down his faded blue jeans.

"I don't think your mum would want the hassle," he said.

"But she asked you over," I reminded him. "On Saturday, after you walked me home?"

"Are you sure?" Gurnam asked.

I nodded.

"OK then," he said. "I like pasta."

3

Back at home, Mum looked worried when she opened the door.

"Has something else happened?" she asked as she looked from me to Gurnam. Her face was creased with concern.

"Nothing's happened!" I told her. "I just bumped into Gurnam and asked him over for tea. Is that OK?"

Mum smiled.

"Of course," she replied. "Welcome, Gurnam. Always happy to make friends with a neighbour. The more, the merrier."

"Who's here?" I asked.

"Olivia and Lola," Mum said. "How are you, Gurnam?"

"Fine," he said. "But I don't want to be a burden. I can just go home."

"Nonsense!" Mum replied. "Besides, the amount of pasta I've made would feed an army."

I pulled a face.

"Mum always makes too much," I joked. "It's like she's obsessed with it. We've got more pasta than the whole of Italy in our house!"

"Well, if you're sure," Gurnam said.

I walked into the living room, where Olivia and Lola were watching telly.

"Hey!" I said to Lola.

"Ssh!" Lola said. "I can't hear the TV!"

As usual, Lola had made herself at home.

"Are those my slippers you're wearing?" I asked her.

Lola looked at her feet and pulled a face.

"I think so," she said. "They're too big for my dainty feet."

Olivia grinned. She was in her fifties, with short, greying blonde hair and pale-blue eyes.

"Ignore Lola and come sit by me," Olivia said. "I haven't seen you since ..."

"Er ... *yesterday?*" I replied.

But I still sank into the huge hug Olivia offered me. She wasn't just Lola's nan – she'd always been my babysitter, too. It was like she was *my* nan – buying me birthday and Christmas presents, and celebrating Diwali with us. I loved her.

"I invited Gurnam over," I told Olivia and Lola.

Olivia raised an eyebrow. She knew about the boys in the park.

"You mean the lovely man who helped you on Saturday?" she said.

I nodded.

"*Oooh!*" Olivia said. "Is he handsome?"

"*Nan!*" Lola groaned. "Don't be so minging! Old people don't do that sort of thing!"

We burst into laughter just as Gurnam and Mum entered the room. Gurnam looked confused and a bit embarrassed, and Mum shook her head.

"Don't worry about these three," Mum told him. "They're always like this."

I watched Olivia glance at Gurnam. Her eyes widened and she smiled.

"Handsome, then?" I whispered to her.

"Ooh la la!" Olivia whispered back. "Welcome to the neighbourhood!"

As the five of us ate at the kitchen table, I kept an eye on Gurnam. He seemed fairly happy, but he didn't fool me. Since Dad went, I had become really good at understanding people's true feelings. It wasn't magic or anything – I just sensed when people tried to hide their emotions. And Gurnam was doing it now. He smiled with his mouth, but his eyes were distant, like he was thinking about something bad. I wondered where he'd lived before he moved to our street. I wondered if he had a family, and why they weren't with him.

"Any seconds for you, Gurnam?" Mum asked, interrupting my thoughts.

"I'm good," he replied. "That was delicious."

"Take some home," Mum urged him. "We've got plenty left over."

"There's a rugby team coming over tomorrow," Olivia joked to Mum. "They'll need feeding too."

Mum picked up a pasta strand and threw it at Olivia. It missed and landed on the floor, where Milly gobbled it up. Lola started to giggle.

"Mum!" I shouted. "Why would you do that?"

"Yes, don't be so childish!" Olivia said, laughing.

Mum groaned, told us to shut up and refilled the adults' wine glasses.

"So, you'll take some pasta home?" Mum said to Gurnam.

"I'm fine, thanks," he replied. "I've got plenty of food at home. Well, in my new house. It's not really *home* ..."

Gurnam gulped and looked away for a moment.

"Where *is* home?" I asked him, being a bit too nosy.

"Aman," Mum said. "Don't pry ..."

"It's fine, Jeet," Gurnam said, and turned to me. "I used to live in Leicester. But then I moved here – a few weeks ago."

I nodded but didn't reply. We lived just outside Leicester, so why had Gurnam moved? Why not just live where you called home?

"My life got a bit ... *complicated*, and I had to leave," Gurnam added, as if he'd read my mind. "Anyway, that's the past. I want to know more about you."

He was changing the subject, but that was fine. I didn't want to upset him. I didn't like upsetting people.

"I don't know what to say," I replied. "I'm just boring ..."

"No, you're not," Mum said. "You're great!"

My face burned with embarrassment.

"*Yeah!*" Lola said. "I'd never have *boring* friends, Aman. I mean, you're a bit weird and you fart a lot, but you're still awesome!"

I glared at Lola and her silliness, but she just stuck out her tongue.

22

"I love my puppy," I said to Gurnam. "And I like art and music and stuff. And Lola can be annoying, but she's really funny and she's been my best friend since forever. Have you got a best friend?"

"Aman!" Mum said.

"It's OK, really," Gurnam told her. "I had one really close friend. But we don't see each other any more. We fell out and ..."

He looked past me and nodded just once.

"Yeah, we fell out," Gurnam repeated. "It's one of those things ..."

"I like football," I blurted out, just to stop him getting gloomy. "Liverpool FC, because Dad ..."

Mum put her hand on my knee as I said Dad's name, but I was OK.

"Dad was a big Liverpool fan," I continued. "I used to watch games with him."

Mum gave a warm smile and told Gurnam, "Aman was three when she got her first football kit. I've still got photos of her in it."

"Liverpool FC, huh?" Gurnam said. "Guess what, kid?"

"What?" I asked.

"Me too!" Gurnam told me. "I love Liverpool. You and I are going to get on just fine."

I smiled because we had something in common. And that was important because I liked Gurnam. He was cool.

"I try to play football sometimes, but I'm rubbish," I said.

"Well," Gurnam said, "we can change that. I'll show you some tricks one day."

"Did you play football?" I asked.

"All the time," he replied. "I'd still play now if I could find some old codgers to play with."

"Old codgers?" I said. I'd never heard that phrase before.

"Ancient rusty men like me," Gurnam said with a wink.

"You're not that old," I said.

"I'm fifty-nine," he told me. "I'll be sixty on Christmas Day."

"Wow, really?" I said. "How cool is that?"

Gurnam smiled properly this time, with his eyes too. Then he looked at his watch.

"I'd better go," he told Mum. "I'm keeping you from your evening ..."

"We're watching a rom-com," Lola said. "And we've got ice cream and popcorn – it's all a bit girly ..."

"Lola!" Olivia said.

Gurnam shrugged, then smiled.

"Well, I'll say good evening, then," he told Lola. "But I do like a good romance now and then. I prefer books to films though."

Gurnam turned to Mum and said, "Thank you for tea. It was very kind, and I appreciate it."

"A pleasure," Mum replied.

"Will you come and see us again?" I asked him.

Gurnam nodded.

"Of course," he said, looking at Mum. "If that's OK with you, Jeet?"

Mum nodded.

"That would be lovely," she replied. "We could share our favourite books, maybe?"

"Great," Gurnam said, and he winked at me. "See you soon."

4

I looked out for Gurnam the following week but didn't see him at all. I started to get worried, even though I knew it was silly. Mum noticed my mood and hugged me when I told her. She explained that Olivia had seen Gurnam, and he'd said that he'd been busy.

"I'm sure he'll pop over soon," Mum added.

That Saturday, Mum and I had a fried breakfast, then walked Milly to the park. It was cold and sunny again, perfect for our Community Garden project. I was wearing tattered old jeans and my orange wellies. Mum wore grey leggings, one of Dad's old hooded tops and his smelly green wellies.

"Remember when we used to garden with Dad?" I said.

"I remember the *mess* you both made," Mum joked. "Leaving mud all over the house."

"We did that on purpose," I teased her. "To wind you up."

"I didn't mind, really," Mum replied, and her eyes welled up.

I took her hand and squeezed it.

"Miss him," I said.

Mum just nodded.

We headed for an abandoned nature reserve in the middle of the park. It had been overgrown and full of rubbish since I'd been small. We were going to rescue it for our Community Garden project. As we arrived, Olivia spotted us. She was wearing black dungarees, brown wellies and a pink bobbled hat.

"Over here, my lovelies!" Olivia said.

She had been digging with a rusty shovel. Her cheeks were flushed and her hands covered in muck.

"Beautiful winter morning," she said. "Perfect for our first day."

Olivia and Mum got chatting, so I took Milly for a walk around the nature reserve. Lots of people were helping out, including some pupils from school and my year head, Mrs West.

"Hello, Aman!" Mrs West said. "How lovely to see you!"

"Hey, miss," I said.

"Oh no," Mrs West said. "We're not in school today. Call me Claire."

She pointed to some litter pickers – long sticks with triggers and grab hands.

"Could you help pick up litter?" Mrs West asked. "We need to clear the area before we begin."

"OK, miss," I replied.

Mrs West grinned and said, "*Claire!* I'm not a teacher at weekends, Aman!"

I grinned back.

"OK, Claire," I said. "Meet Milly ..."

Milly yapped as Mrs West tickled her and said, "She's adorable!"

The problem was, I couldn't help with Milly in tow. Bringing her along had been silly.

"Back to the house for you," I said to Milly as an idea formed in my mind.

Milly seemed happy to be home. She darted into her pen in the kitchen and sniffed her smelly cushion. Soon, she'd settled down next to her food, water and toys. As I locked the gate, she whimpered a bit but then closed her eyes.

"See you later!" I said.

But instead of going back to the nature reserve, I went to Gurnam's house. He lived a few doors away from ours, past Olivia's. I walked up the path feeling nervous and knocked on his door. After a moment, I rang the bell. Then I tried again, but he didn't answer.

Maybe he wasn't in, I told myself. Or maybe he wanted to be left alone. I knew how that felt sometimes. It was no big deal. Only, the gate at the side of the house was ajar.

"Hmmm ..." I said aloud.

I went over and pushed the gate wide open. The passage alongside the house was like ours: a narrow paved walkway that led to the garden. I thought about leaving, but I was too curious. I walked towards Gurnam's garden, praying that he wouldn't find me and be annoyed.

That was when I heard him sobbing. My heart sank. As I reached the garden, I saw Gurnam sitting on a chair with his back to me. He was all alone and drinking from a bottle of booze. I thought about calling out but didn't.

"I'm sorry!" he said to no one – he didn't know I was there. "I'm sorry. If I could change who I am, I would!"

I felt awful for spying on Gurnam. Especially after he'd been so kind to me. I thought about someone watching me when I felt sad or when I was alone in my room, whispering to Dad. I would have been gutted.

I turned and walked away as fast as I could.

5

That night, I struggled to sleep. I kept wondering why Gurnam was so sad. I wanted to tell him that I understood. That it's OK to be sad. But I felt really guilty too. I shouldn't have gone to his house. I shouldn't have watched him like that.

Eventually, I got up and found my letter to Dad. I read it a few times, and it made me cry. The world seemed so unfair. Dad was kind and thoughtful, and funny and caring. It didn't seem right that he was gone. I wanted to watch Liverpool FC games with him again. I wanted to hug him and call him smelly. After a while, I went back to sleep, but I kept waking up as I thought about everything Dad had taught me.

Mum was up bright and early the next morning.

"It's day two!" she said in the kitchen as I yawned over my cereal and toast.

"Huh?" I said.

"The project?" Mum replied.

"Oh ..."

She sat down and looked into my eyes.

"Bad night?" Mum asked.

"Yeah," I told her.

I wanted to explain about Gurnam, but I couldn't. I was just too ashamed of myself. And I didn't want Mum to be ashamed of me too.

"You don't have to come along," Mum told me. "You helped yesterday."

I shook my head.

"No," I replied. "I'm OK. I just need to wake up a bit."

"If you're sure," Mum said.

I nodded.

I was in the nature reserve an hour later when Lola surprised me.

"Hey, bum face!" she yelled as I helped with the weeding.

"What are you doing here?" I asked, feeling relieved to see her. If anyone could help my mood, it was Lola.

"I volunteered in secret," she said. "It was Nan's idea – we wanted to surprise you."

"Gold star for effort!" I said. "You got me."

Soon we were working, chatting and enjoying ourselves. We even forgot about lunch until Mum turned up with crisps and sandwiches and fruity water. Lola and I walked to the fenced-off play area, sat on a bench and started eating. We were talking about Lola's latest favourite book when something landed by my feet – a half-eaten pasty.

"Who just ...?" I began, but I should have known.

The two lads who had attacked Milly stood at the railings to the play area. They were wearing the same outfits as before.

"It's Little Miss Cry Baby and her ugly friend," the smaller lad said.

"Get lost!" Lola shouted.

"What you doin' over there?" the taller lad asked, and he nodded at the nature reserve.

I shrugged. "It's the Community Garden project," I replied, thinking he might really be interested.

"What – you planting flowers and shit?"

I didn't reply.

"How messed up is that?" the tall lad said. "Ain't you got better things to do?"

"It's called *helping the neighbourhood*," Lola told him. "You wouldn't know what that means."

The tall one laughed, and he reminded me of a goat again.

"I help out, plenty," he said. "Like, now I'm gonna take your money and your phones and donate them to the poor."

"We're the poor," the small spotty boy said. "They call it *redistribution*, y'know. Learned that in college."

The taller one grinned and said, "Bruv, you ain't never in college! What you know 'bout economics an' that?"

They jumped over the railings and walked towards us.

"We haven't got anything," Lola shouted.

I could tell she was afraid – her leg trembled against mine. I was scared too. My mouth went dry, and my stomach was in knots. I thought about grabbing Lola and running, but it wouldn't help. They would easily catch us. I gulped down air. What were we going to do?

"*Aman?*" I heard Gurnam shout.

My eyes widened. Gurnam was standing by the gate of the play area. He'd saved me again, like my own personal superhero. The lads saw him too.

"It's the Return of Granddad!" the shorter one mocked him. "Help, help!"

Gurnam walked over with a hard, stony face.

"Last chance," he warned the lads. "You should be ashamed – picking on kids. Pick on *me*, I *dare* you ..."

He rolled up the sleeves of his tatty green jumper. His hands tightened into huge fists, and I saw his forearms had tattoos on them. I couldn't see the detail, but I *could* see the muscles.

"Come on, then," Gurnam said softly. "You're not scared of an old man, are you?"

The smaller one tensed, as if to fight, but the taller boy held him back.

"Broad daylight, innit?" he said to Gurnam. "Witnesses too. Man ain't gettin' arrested. Ain't that dumb."

"*Really?*" Gurnam asked. "You harass children, but you're not stupid? I reckon you need a dictionary, son."

"I ain't your son," the taller one said. "You is too ugly."

He looked around, then tugged his friend's arm and said, "Come, bruv. We'll catch this dickhead another day."

"Any time," Gurnam said. "Now, get lost. If I catch you bothering Aman again, I'll knock you out."

The smaller lad spat close to Gurnam's feet and said, "I *know* about you."

Gurnam froze and seemed lost for a moment. But then he snapped out of it.

"You don't know anything about me," he replied.

"Whatever you say, innit?" the smaller one said.

The lads started laughing and walked away without looking back. Gurnam rolled down his sleeves and grinned at me and Lola.

"Hello again," he said. "Got a sandwich for me, too?"

If I had smiled any wider, I might have blinded someone.

6

Gurnam became a regular visitor to our house after rescuing me the second time. And he seemed to grow closer to Olivia, too. A couple of Fridays later, Gurnam and Olivia both came for supper. I watched them chatting and wondered what Lola would think. Some Friday night, she would say. Stuck at home listening to a couple of old people flirting. You might as well watch *Antiques Roadshow*. I thought I'd find it weird too, but it wasn't.

Gurnam was having fun. He was smiling and joking. His eyes weren't quite calm yet, but I was getting used to that. After how I'd seen him in his garden, I was just happy he looked so relaxed.

"I bet you're bored," Olivia said to me. "Hanging about with us oldies. You should've asked Lola to stay."

I shook my head.

"Nah, you're OK," I said. "It's like having a live museum exhibit in my house. You know, how people lived in *ye olden days* ..."

"You cheeky little moo!" Olivia spluttered.

Gurnam laughed, then pulled a face and pointed at the sink.

"Speaking of old," Gurnam said. "Is your tap leaking, Jeet?"

Mum shrugged.

"Yeah," she said. "It's been like that for a long time."

Gurnam went over to the sink to investigate. He turned the tap on and off, then wiggled it a bit. I joined him.

"Did your father keep any tools?" he said.

I poked his arm, and he pulled a face.

"That's sexist," I told Gurnam. "Mum has tools."

"Whoops," he said, and looked sheepish. "I didn't mean ..."

"They're under the stairs," I said. "Mum doesn't exactly use them ..."

"Go and get them," Gurnam said. "I'll fix it."

Ten minutes later, the tap was in bits and Gurnam looked annoyed.

"I need a washer," he told me.

"What's that?" I asked.

He held up a small rubber ring. It had snapped.

"This," Gurnam told me. "It stops water from leaking past the valve when the tap is closed. We need a fresh one."

I had no idea what a *valve* was, but I didn't tell him.

"Don't think Mum has one of them," I replied. "She's just a *girl* ..."

Gurnam laughed again.

"Guess I deserve that," he told me. "I've got some spare washers at home. I'll just go and get one."

Ten minutes later, the tap was like new. As Gurnam put the tools away, he spotted something else.

"That door's hanging off too," he said.

Mum smiled and told him, "Everything's old in here. To be honest, we need a new kitchen. I just don't have time to find someone to fit it."

She was right. The kitchen *was* falling apart. The cupboards were chipped and cracked, and the worktops were scratched. Plus there was a musty smell – like mould and rubbish – coming from the sink.

"I'll do it," Gurnam said.

"*Ooh!*" Olivia said. "I do like a handy man!"

Olivia and I burst into giggles, and Gurnam looked confused.

"I'm a builder," Gurnam explained. "At least, I used to be."

"Really?" Mum asked. "You mean, you could fit a new kitchen?"

Gurnam laughed.

"I could build you a new *house*," he told her. "Kitchens are easy."

"But would you want to?" Mum said. "I'd pay you, of course."

Gurnam looked at me and shrugged.

"Tell you what," he said. "You buy the materials, and I'll do the rest."

"But I don't want to impose ..." Mum began.

"I'm happy to help," said Gurnam. "Besides, it will give me something to do."

I turned to Mum and gave her a pleading look. But I didn't need to convince her. She was grinning.

"You're on!" Mum said.

Mum didn't mess about. She wanted the kitchen done for Christmas, which was just a few weeks away. By Sunday night, she and Gurnam had ordered the new stuff online. And soon our old kitchen was gone. We had to eat at Olivia's house all week, but I didn't mind, especially as Lola kept turning up. Gurnam seemed to enjoy working on the kitchen, and Olivia spent all week chatting to him and making tea. I thought they made the perfect couple.

On the Friday night, Gurnam took me to the chip shop.

"Thank you," he said to me as we walked home with our food.

"What for?" I asked. It was so cold that my nose was running.

"Just ..."

He looked away and gulped. I sniffed and waited for him to continue.

"You've been so generous," he said at last. "Your mum and Olivia, too. I don't know where I would be if ..."

We didn't say anything for a moment. Then I sniffed again and wished I had a tissue.

"We like you," I told him. "You're lovely and kind and fun to be around. Like a granddad."

As soon as I spoke, I regretted it. Sometimes your inner thoughts should stay private. Like, people can't handle them – especially adults. At least, that was what I thought. But Gurnam just stopped and smiled. He didn't look embarrassed or freaked out or anything.

"Granddad's fine by me," he told me.

My eyes welled up with tears.

"Dad died," I blurted out.

"I know," Gurnam said. "I guessed."

"He died and I needed him and ..." I couldn't go on.

Gurnam squeezed my hand. He smelled of sawdust and plaster, and I remembered how Dad held me when I was unhappy. How he made everything seem fine. My eyes welled up again, and I could feel my chin wobbling.

"Sorry ..." I said, and wiped away at my eyes. "I'm being stupid ..."

"It's not stupid at all." Gurnam sighed. "People are supposed to cry if they're sad."

I pulled away and looked at him. I thought of that day I saw him in his garden. But I still couldn't tell him that I'd seen him crying.

"Do you cry?" I asked him. "I mean, I can tell that you're unhappy. It's in your eyes, even when you laugh."

Gurnam nodded slowly.

"I get low sometimes," he said. "I feel numb, like there's nothing inside me. But being around your lovely family and friends makes me *feel* something ..."

"That makes me happy," I told him.

"Me too," said Gurnam.

We walked the rest of the way in silence.

7

The following day, Lola's eyes widened when I told her what Gurnam had said. We were taking a break at the Community Garden project. It was a grey, cold day, and my hands were frozen.

"What do you mean he *feels* something?" Lola asked. "Does Gurnam fancy Nan?"

"I'm not sure," I said. "But they'd make a cool couple."

I told Lola that Olivia and Gurnam had been flirting at my house all week. Lola threw her hand over her mouth and laughed.

"But Nan hasn't ever had a boyfriend," she replied. "Not since my granddad left."

Olivia and Lola's granddad had split up a few years earlier.

"Your nan could have a boyfriend now," I said, making Lola wince.

"*Euurrrgh!*" Lola groaned. "That's just *weird*!"

"Why?"

"Old people, doing kissy stuff!" she replied. "That's just not right."

I shook my head.

"They aren't old people," I told her. "They're human beings."

"Wrinkly, *old* human beings," Lola joked. "God, can you imagine them kissing? Yuck!"

She pulled another face, and I poked her arm.

"Don't be so mean," I said. "They're perfect for each other."

Lola smiled and said, "OK, then. Are we gonna fix them up?"

I nodded.

"How?" Lola asked.

"I don't know," I replied. "But it'll be fun trying!"

By the evening, we had a plan. And when I got home, Gurnam was still working on the kitchen.

"Just finished the new plaster," he told me and Mum. "I should be able to start the cupboards tomorrow."

He wore protective goggles and overalls that were covered in dust.

"But tomorrow is Sunday," I told him. "You can't work on a Sunday."

"It's no big deal," Gurnam said, taking off his goggles. "I don't mind."

"But I need your help," I told him. "To practise my football skills."

He smiled, but Mum shook her head at me.

"I'm sure Gurnam doesn't want to spend *every* day with us," she said. "Don't pressure him, Aman."

"No, no," said Gurnam. "I've got no plans."

Gurnam worked on the kitchen on Sunday morning but walked me to the park after lunch. It was all part of my plan.

"Play with your head up," Gurnam said as he kicked the football to me. "So that you know what's going on."

"But how will I see the ball?" I asked.

"You get used to it," he replied. "Just try."

I really welcomed his help. I wanted to play for my school team but wasn't very good. I did as Gurnam said, but I felt like a baby giraffe on an ice rink.

"I'm useless!" I said.

"If you tell yourself that," Gurnam said, "you'll never improve. Come on, keep at it!"

I tried again, over and over, until I actually got better.

"See?" Gurnam said. "Now, how about passing?"

But I'd spotted Olivia and Lola walking towards us. Olivia was wearing a red coat with a matching scarf and hat, and she looked great. Perfect for our plan. Lola grinned and waved.

"Oh, look who it is!" I said, picking up the ball.

Gurnam turned and saw them.

"Fancy meeting you here," Olivia said.

Lola winked at me and said, "*Yeah. Imagine that?*" I winced – she was being way too obvious.

"We're practising football," I said quickly. "Gurnam is a great coach."

Olivia looked impressed. I watched her eyes sparkle. She liked Gurnam, I was sure of it.

"You're a man of many talents," Olivia said.

"It's nothing," Gurnam replied. "Just a few tips."

"We're going for tea and cake," Lola said. "Why don't you join us?"

"That would be lovely," Olivia said.

Gurnam didn't look so sure. He eyed the ball and then me.

"What about football?" he asked.

"It's no problem," I told him. "We can come back another day. The girls' team doesn't play again until after Christmas. We've got plenty of time."

It was getting colder, and huge dark rainclouds loomed above us.

"Well," Gurnam said, "as long as Olivia doesn't mind."

"Of course not," Olivia said with a smile. "Come on."

The coffee shop was on the high street. It was busy and warm, and the windows steamy. The coffee smell inside reminded me of Dad, and I actually smiled. Normally, thinking of Dad made me want to cry, but something about today made me feel cosy instead. As we sat down, Olivia asked what we were having.

"Oh, I nearly forgot!" Lola said. "We need to get a birthday present for this girl at school."

"Really?" Olivia asked.

"Er ... yeah," I said.

"The gift shop is open," Lola added. "Aman and I will go and buy something, then meet you back here."

"Oh, OK then," Olivia said. "Shall I order for you, so that your drinks are ready when you get back?"

"No hurry!" Lola said. "We can order later."

Once we were outside, Lola squealed with delight.

"It worked!" she said. "It actually worked!"

"You cheeky monkeys!" Olivia said to us when we got home. She was sitting at our kitchen table having a cup of tea with Mum. "Setting me and Gurnam up on a date!"

"Sorry," I replied. "I just thought you'd make a great couple. And you always flirt with each other."

"It was just a bit of fun, Nan!" Lola said.

Olivia picked up one of Gurnam's work gloves that he'd left on the table.

"Gurnam's lovely," she told us. "But he's not my type."

"Oh!" I said, feeling disappointed.

"And, more importantly," Olivia added, "I'm *definitely* not his."

So much for my great plan.

8

The kitchen was finished by mid-December. It looked wonderful, with cream cupboards and real wooden worktops. Everything was shiny and new, and the bad smell was gone. But when Mum tried to pay Gurnam, he just shook his head.

"No need," he said. "It gave me a reason to be."

I didn't really understand what he meant, but I could guess. Mum wasn't happy though.

"Absolutely not," she told Gurnam in a stern voice. "You *will* take some money."

Gurnam burst into laughter.

"I said no," he replied. "You've been so good to me. It's the least I could do."

They argued some more, but in the end Gurnam gave in. Mum is pretty good at winning arguments – trust me.

"And you'll eat Christmas dinner with us, too," Mum added. "No excuses."

Gurnam nodded but didn't look that keen.

"I normally spend Christmas alone," he replied softly. "It's a difficult time for me."

I put my hand on his arm.

"That's why you should be with us," I told him. "That's what friends are for."

"You're more than friends," Gurnam told me. "You're family."

That lunchtime, Mum took me to a Sikh temple – called a *gurdwara*. I wanted to help at the Community Garden project, but Mum insisted I go with her to the gurdwara.

"My friend is having a blessing there for her daughter's birthday," Mum told me.

"Do I *have* to go?" I asked.

"Yes," Mum said. "It would be rude not to."

She parked in the gurdwara's car park. As I got out, I saw a tall flagpole in front of the building. The pole had been wrapped in orange fabric, and the Sikh flag was orange too, with a black oval symbol.

"We won't stay long," Mum said.

"OK," I said.

When I'd been younger, we'd hardly ever visited the gurdwara. Mum and Dad had never been religious. And since Dad had gone, Mum and I went just once or twice a year. Inside, we covered our heads, removed our shoes and went into the main prayer room. A platform in the middle was covered in a canopy of gold and scarlet fabric. A priest sat behind it, reading from a copy of the Sikh holy book. It was peaceful and calm, and the air smelt of rose incense.

We went up to the platform, knelt down and bowed. Then we threw money into a collection box. After we'd sat for about fifteen minutes, Mum gestured for us to leave. Another priest gave us some *prashad* – a sticky, sweet baked mix of flour, butter and sugar. It looked greasy, but it tasted amazing.

"Wow!" I whispered as we left. "I forgot how tasty this stuff is!"

"It is," Mum agreed.

Mum's friend was in the dining hall. Every Sikh temple has one, so that people can eat *langar* – a free meal. Mum was busy chatting to people, but I wasn't in the mood to talk. I said hello but didn't get involved in their conversations. I wasn't bored, exactly. I just got lost in my own head. I wanted to be alone. The prayer room had been calm, but the dining hall was crowded, with nowhere to hide. I started to feel anxious and looked for an escape.

I went outside for some fresh air. A group of teenage lads stood by the entrance, their heads covered with white handkerchiefs. As I passed by, I saw one of them was the small spotty idiot from the park. Thankfully, he didn't see me. I hurried past and hid behind a white van. The lads were loud, and I could hear every word they were saying. I soon realised who they were talking about, too. *Gurnam* ...

"Man's giving it the large one," the lad from the park said. "Like I don't know who he is."

"Everyone knows that prick, you get me, Sunny?" another lad said.

So the spotty lad's name was Sunny.

"Seen him twice now," Sunny said, "hanging out with some young girl. I should punch him, innit."

"If that was *my* kid," another lad said, "I'd keep her away."

Why were they being so mean about Gurnam, I wondered. He wasn't nasty. He was kind and generous and caring.

"I heard he dumped his family," one lad said. "Like, at *his* age ..."

"Just wrong," Sunny added. "Against nature, innit? Real men don't do that nastiness!"

"Left his wife and kids," his mate said. "Even had grandchildren, too!"

I couldn't listen to any more. I walked around the building to a side entrance and found Mum in the gurdwara. She was drinking tea and eating a samosa.

"I need to leave," I whispered.

"Pardon?" Mum said.

"Please, Mum!" I pleaded. "I'm not feeling well. Can we leave?"

Mum looked into my eyes and saw my distress.

"Oh, *Aman*," she said.

She gave me a hug, made her excuses to her friend and we left.

At home, I went straight to bed, but I couldn't sleep. The same questions spun around in my mind. Had Gurnam done something bad? And what sort of man left his family like that? Maybe Gurnam wasn't what he seemed. Maybe he was just putting on an act. Was he lying to me and Mum?

And then I felt guilty for listening to idiot lads gossiping. I re-read my letter to Dad a few times. Then I lay back and remembered Dad's scent when he'd been cooking – curry spices and beer. I thought about his smile – how it lit up his entire face. I just wanted to hold his hand again.

"Wish you were still here," I whispered.

9

I woke up the next morning feeling dazed. Milly got excited when I opened my eyes. But I didn't play with her. I wanted to hide under my pillow and sleep for ever. I felt cold and empty inside. When Mum knocked on my door, I wasn't pleased.

"You need to talk to me," Mum said. "What's going on?"

"Leave me alone!" I replied. "I don't *want* to talk."

Mum knew my moods, so she left. But ten minutes later I went downstairs to apologise to her.

"I'm sorry," I said. "I just ..."

"Something happened yesterday, didn't it?" Mum said.

"Yeah," I replied. "I was thinking about Dad, and I got all upset and I ..."

Mum put her arms around me.

"You don't apologise for feeling sad," she told me. "Not ever. But you have to try to talk about it."

"I know," I replied. "But there's something else too ..."

"What's that?" Mum asked.

I didn't know how to begin. Why had I believed what Sunny had said? Why was I taking his word over Gurnam's kindness? Gurnam had been generous and caring since we'd met. Why would I doubt him now?

"Aman?" Mum asked.

"I heard some lads talking about Gurnam," I admitted. "At the gurdwara. They said he was a bad man."

Mum was shocked.

"What lads?" she said.

"Just some boys," I replied.

"And what did they say?"

"That Gurnam left his family because he did something bad," I told Mum. "They said he was nasty and ..."

Mum put her hands around my face.

"Why would you listen to strangers gossiping?" she asked me. "We know that Gurnam has a past, Aman. We know that he has problems."

"But ..." I started.

"No," Mum said softly. "Listen to me, OK? Gurnam has been nothing but wonderful with us."

"But what kind of person just leaves their family?" I said.

"An *unhappy* person?" Mum suggested. "Someone with depression. Someone who needs to move on?"

I thought about her words for a moment.

"Gurnam's past is *his* business," Mum continued. "We have no right to judge him. Whatever happened, he must have his reasons."

"But we should ask him," I replied. "We should make sure ..."

"Even if that upsets him?" Mum asked.

"I don't know!" I said. "I'm just so *confused*."

Mum took hold of my hand. It was how she always calmed me down.

"Gurnam told me," Mum revealed.

"Told you what?"

"About his family," she said. "He told me in confidence, Aman, and I couldn't break his trust to tell you."

I couldn't believe what I was hearing.

"You *knew*?" I said.

"Kind of," Mum told me. "But only that he left. He didn't say why."

"But what about his family?"

Mum sighed.

"Gurnam has a big family – a wife and adult children, and grandkids, too. He left last year and went away. He didn't tell me where."

My mind started racing with what might have happened. Why had Gurnam left? What if he really was a bad person? He could have been to prison or something. That might explain why he'd gone away …

"So, we should ask him," I said. "We have to ask him, don't we?"

Mum shrugged and said, "I don't know. We don't know Gurnam's reasons for leaving. And he has a right to his privacy. We all have secrets, Aman. Maybe he'd like to keep his?"

Maybe he did, but that didn't stop me wanting to know. Did that make me a bad person?

Later that afternoon, Gurnam was laughing and joking with Olivia at the Community Garden project. The nature reserve looked amazing, although there was still a lot to do. The pond had been cleared and re-done, and new shrubs and flowers had been planted everywhere. We had one more week until the re-opening.

But I didn't care. I was too busy trying to spot something different about Gurnam. I felt terrible – the worst friend in the world – but I couldn't help it. Gurnam soon realised something was wrong.

"Aman ...?" Gurnam said. "Are you OK?"

I had two choices. Carry on ignoring the difficult stuff or deal with it. I was tired of ignoring things, so I chose to deal with it. I didn't think, I didn't consider my words. I just reacted to Gurnam's question. And I shouldn't have ...

"You left your family," I said.

Gurnam's expression changed from concern to surprise.

"I'm sorry?" he said.

"Your family," I repeated. "Your wife and children and *grandchildren* ..."

"Who told you that?" he said.

He didn't seem annoyed or angry. He just looked drained. His broad shoulders slumped, and his pale-brown eyes glazed over.

"Is it true?" I asked.

He nodded.

"Why didn't you tell me?" I asked.

Gurnam gulped and looked away. Three of my school friends were planting flowers by the pond. Lola and Olivia were spreading mulch in a bed of bushes. Two small kids ran around, playing tag and yelling with delight. It was a lovely cold Sunday afternoon. You could almost smell Christmas coming, but there was no festive cheer between me and Gurnam.

"My reasons for leaving are mine alone," Gurnam said. "What others think about that is up to them ..."

"I don't understand," I admitted.

"I couldn't stay, so I left," Gurnam explained. "I think I did the right thing. But the people I left behind felt hurt and betrayed. They see my actions in a different way."

I noticed that he had called them *people*. Not his *family*, not his *loved ones*. Just *people* ...

"Gurnam ..." I began.

"I think about it every day," he cut me off. "And I'm *tired*, Aman. I'm tired of life. Sometimes I just want to go away for ever ..."

My stomach churned with fear. What did he mean by that?

"But I'm here!" I insisted. "You can talk to me and Mum. You don't have to hide from us. We ..."

"I can't talk about it," Gurnam told me. "There's no space in my head for this, Aman. For *any* of this ..."

He turned and walked away. My stomach sank, and my heart began to ache.

"Gurnam!" I called after him, but he ignored me.

I stood and watched, and forced myself not to cry. I felt terrible for upsetting him.

"Please, Gurnam!" I shouted.

But he didn't look back – he didn't even pause. He just trudged away.

10

Lola took hold of my hand as we sat outside the chip shop after school on Monday. Her fingers were long and slim, the nails painted in clear varnish.

"Can I be honest?" Lola asked me.

I heard a police siren shriek in the distance. It was really cold, but I didn't feel a thing.

"Erm ... OK?" I replied.

"You won't get mad?"

I shook my head.

Lola took a breath and said, "Maybe you're, like, confusing your feelings about your dad with Gurnam? And that's why you're so upset?"

I thought about it for a moment. But I didn't agree.

"No," I said. "I *know* I'm messed up from losing Dad. *Everyone* knows I'm messed up, but ..."

"You're not messed up!" Lola interrupted. She sounded annoyed. "Don't you dare say that!"

"I am," I insisted. "It's a fact."

"No," Lola said. "You're dealing with something difficult, that's all. It's natural."

"But it's been a long time," I replied, "since Dad ... *went*."

I still couldn't say *died* aloud – not to Mum or anyone. Only Gurnam had heard me use that word. That had to mean something, didn't it?

"Who cares how long it's been?" said Lola. "It's not a competition to see who recovers the fastest."

I shrugged and said to her, "I promise I'm not confusing the Gurnam situation with Dad. I'm just worried I've hurt Gurnam, and he's important to me. I *have* to know if he's OK."

"He'll forgive you," Lola told me. "He will ..."

But I wasn't so sure he would. We hadn't seen him for two days, and that was weird. I'd grown used to having Gurnam around. Drinking tea in the new kitchen or watching telly with Olivia and Mum. He had become part of our lives.

And I had screwed that up.

The week went on, and by Thursday evening we were decorating the Community Garden for Christmas. My cold mood matched the freezing weather, but that didn't stop me from helping. Our entire neighbourhood had joined in, even people who hadn't been involved before. Olivia and Mum were placing wooden reindeer and elves around the garden, and Lola and I draped them in tinsel. Meanwhile, other pupils from our school worked on a nativity scene, and the guys from the chip shop were stringing up fairy lights.

After we'd finished hanging the tinsel, Mrs West called us over.

"I need your help," she said.

Mrs West pointed to some mini Christmas trees. They were about a metre high and undecorated.

"We need to plant those trees," she explained, "and place them around the garden."

Lola seemed confused and said, "But they're *fake*. How can we plant fake trees?"

Mrs West laughed.

"With some Christmas elf magic!" she joked.

Mrs West showed us a stack of brown plant pots. Beside them were pieces of foam, cut so that they would fit neatly into the pots. A wheelbarrow nearby was loaded with a big bag of white gravel.

"First, we're going to pack each pot with foam," Mrs West told us.

We followed her instructions, taking a pot each and filling it with foam. Meanwhile, Mrs West carefully inserted a metal spike into the base of each tree.

"There you go!" she said, and pushed a tree into my pot. The spike at the bottom secured the tree to the foam.

"Now we cover the foam with white gravel and we're set!" Mrs West said.

"And tinsel," Lola said. "We have to use tinsel."

Mrs West nodded.

"Absolutely," she said. "We've even got fake snow spray!"

We spent another half an hour decorating our trees and spraying them with fake snow. By the end, they looked cool. As we tidied up, others began to set out the finished trees. The project looked incredible, and everything was perfect – from the nature reserve to the Christmas garden and the nativity scene.

"Wow!" Lola said. "I'm pretty proud of this, aren't you?"

I nodded, but I'd been distracted by something. Gurnam was standing by the pond, chatting to someone. He turned and saw me. But instead of coming across, he looked away. That stung, but I was happy to see Gurnam, anyway. I wanted to go over, but something stopped me.

Lola and I went over to Mum. She was by the nativity scene, chatting to the vicar from our local church.

"Can we go now?" I asked. "I'm cold."

Mum nodded.

"I'll be a couple of minutes," she said. "Why don't you see if Olivia has finished?"

Lola's nan was putting rubbish into black bags when we found her.

"Go back to mine," Olivia suggested, handing us her key. "I'll just get rid of these bags and catch you up."

"Can you tell Mum we've gone?" I asked.

"No problem," Olivia said.

As we left the park, I saw Gurnam again. He was walking just in front of us, and I caught him up. Lola hung back, to give us some privacy.

"Hello," I said.

Gurnam nodded but didn't reply.

"Are you angry with me?" I asked.

"No," he replied. "I'm not angry, Aman – just sad. It's my own fault. I shouldn't have got involved with your family."

"No, I'm the one who should be sorry," I began. "I …"

"I don't want to talk any more," Gurnam told me. "Not to anyone. I just want to be alone."

He walked off at speed, but I didn't follow. Lola caught me up.

"He's still upset?" she asked.

"Yeah," I told her. "He's more than upset, actually. I think I've ruined everything. Why did I open my big mouth?"

Lola linked arms with me.

"Just give him time," she said. "It's Christmas next week. Everything will be fine."

I shook my head and replied, "I don't think it will."

I should have tried harder. I should have made Gurnam listen. Maybe I could have prevented what came next. Things were about to get much, much worse.

11

The next day was the last day of school before Christmas. It was boring – the best part was watching *Scrooge* after lunch. At home time, Lola wanted to hang out, but I wasn't in the mood. My eyes hurt and my brain felt like mush. I just wanted to lie in bed and cuddle Milly.

Just after seven o'clock, Mum and I walked to the chip shop. I was feeling a bit better and looking forward to supper. As usual, some lads from school were hanging about. A couple of them smiled at me, and I smiled back. The chip shop was packed, and the queue ran outside. After we'd stood there for a few minutes, Sunny and his tall mate came out of the off-licence next door. They were carrying tiny vodka bottles and looked drunk. My stomach contracted with fear.

"S'cuse me," Sunny said to Mum.

Mum looked confused.

"I'm sorry," she said. "Are you talking to us?"

"Yeah, I am," Sunny said.

He was wearing a black hoodie, beanie hat and jeans, with red trainers and grey gloves. His breath stank of alcohol.

"Well, I don't want to talk to you," Mum said. "Go away."

Sunny looked at me and grinned. "This your kid, yeah?"

Mum moved to shield me, tense and angry. "I said go away," she told him.

"Don't get hype, lady," Sunny told Mum. "I was just *aksing*, innit?"

As he said *asking* wrong, he swayed a bit. Mum shoved me further towards the chip-shop door.

"Just go away," Mum said. "Before I get really angry. You should be ashamed – harassing women in public. I could be your mother!"

"Hey," Sunny said, a bit too loudly. He seemed almost hurt by Mum's words. "I ain't no weirdo. I just wanna warn you about that nonce your daughter hangs with."

"How dare you?!" Mum began, but Sunny didn't listen.

"That man is *wrong*, you get me?" he continued. "Best keep your kids away from him."

"Maybe we sorted it for you?" Sunny's tall friend said.

"What do you mean?" I asked.

"Be quiet!" Mum told me. "I'll deal with this."

I saw the owner of the chip shop, Mario, duck under the counter. He was short and wide, with huge muscles and a shaved head. His fists were clenched at his sides, and he looked furious.

"Mum ...?" I said.

"Sssh," she replied.

"Just take the warning, innit," Sunny said. "Ain't mean no disrespect ..."

"Everything you've said is disrespectful," Mum told him.

She didn't get to finish, because Mario stepped outside. A couple of customers followed him.

"You OK, Jeet?" Mario asked Mum.

"I'm fine," Mum told him.

Mario turned to the lads.

"Stop bothering my regulars," he said. "You're out here all the time, causing trouble ..."

"What you gonna do about it?" the taller lad asked, but he didn't sound as arrogant now. He looked wary of Mario. He should have been.

Mario grabbed hold of his jacket and said, "Do you really wanna know?"

"Gerroff!" the lad yelped. "That's assault, innit?"

Mario grabbed Sunny with his other hand. Then he pushed both lads along the pavement. The lads were scrawny, and Mario had no trouble shifting them.

"Next time," Mario warned them, "I'll get really angry. Now leave!"

Sunny and his friend skulked away, muttering threats. Mario didn't move until they were long gone.

"You didn't have to do that, Mario," Mum said. "They might report you to the police."

Mario shrugged and smiled.

"For defending my customers and my business?" he said. "Good luck to them. You OK?"

"Yeah," Mum said. "Thanks."

"Now, two haddock and chips, and a large curry sauce, right?" Mario asked.

"And pickled onions," I said.

"Of course, Aman," Mario replied. "Your favourite ..."

On the way home, I told Mum the truth.

"Those lads were the ones who attacked Milly," I said. "When I first met Gurnam."

"That was *them*?" Mum said, and her face grew hard.

"Yeah," I replied. "And the small one was at the gurdwara last week."

"The one who was talking about Gurnam?"

I nodded.

"Do you know his name?" Mum asked.

"Sunny," I said. "So, do we tell the police?"

Mum shook her head.

"No, they can't do anything," she said. "Besides, that's plenty of drama for one night."

But more drama was coming. Five minutes later, as we approached our front door, Olivia hurried towards us.

"Thank God!" Olivia said. "I called you, but you didn't reply!"

She was flustered and frowning, her cheeks pink.

"What's the matter?" Mum asked, checking her bag. "Oh, I think I left my phone at home."

I got a chill but not because of the weather. Something was wrong.

"It's Gurnam!" Olivia said.

Scientists say that the Earth spins at one thousand miles per hour, yet we can't feel it. But as soon as I heard Gurnam's name, I felt it. The ground turned to jelly under my feet. I began to stumble.

"Aman!" Olivia cried, and grabbed hold of me.

Mum took hold of me, too. And between them they started fussing.

"I'm OK," I told them, taking deep breaths. "What's happened to Gurnam?"

Olivia looked from me to Mum.

"Just tell us," Mum said. "It's OK."

"Gurnam was beaten up in the park," Olivia said.

I burst into tears.

"Is he badly hurt?" Mum asked.

"I don't know," Olivia said. "There's an ambulance and police cars ..."

Mum held me tighter and said, "Right. Let's get you inside first."

"No!" I yelled. "I want to see Gurnam!"

Mum took my face in her hands.

"You will listen to me, young lady," she replied. "No arguments!"

She left me at home, grabbed her phone and keys and ran to the park. I sat in the living room, ignoring our fish and chips, still in the bag. My legs wouldn't stop shaking. Milly padded around, but even she seemed subdued. It was like Milly could sense my mood. After a while, she lay down by my feet and closed her eyes.

I turned on the television but couldn't watch anything. Then I tried reading a book but couldn't focus. I didn't want to be at home. I wanted to be in the park. I wanted to be with Gurnam …

The doorbell rang. Lola stood on the doorstep, looking tearful and cold.

"What are you doing here?" I asked as she came in.

"I went to the park after school," Lola told me. "With Mia and Natalia."

They were both in our year – Lola was friends with them.

"I wanted to show them the Community Garden project," Lola continued. "But when we got there, we found Gurnam."

"*You* found him?" I asked.

Lola nodded and started to cry again.

"He ... he ... was just lying on the ground. There was blood everywhere, and a couple of joggers were trying to help him. The nativity scene had been smashed up too. It's ruined!"

"Forget about the project!" I replied. "Tell me about Gurnam."

"He's badly hurt," Lola said. "He wasn't conscious when we ..."

I didn't hear any more. My ears popped and my head throbbed and I couldn't control my churning stomach. I ran to the toilet and puked.

12

The next morning, Mum woke me up. But I wasn't in the mood. I felt numb and tired. Even Milly stayed away, lying in the corner and just watching me.

"I don't want the world today," I said to Mum. "Make it go away."

Mum sat and stroked my hair.

"But I thought you could visit Gurnam," she said.

I looked up.

"What do you think?" Mum added.

I sat up and nodded.

"Is he badly hurt?" I asked her.

"Pretty badly, but he'll be OK," Mum said. "They did some scans yesterday, and he was lucky. He's battered and bruised, and his nose is broken. But he should recover."

I shuddered at the thought of Gurnam in pain.

"Did the police catch his attackers?" I asked.

"Not yet," Mum said. "They're treating it as a hate crime."

"A hate crime?" I said. "Because he's Asian?"

Mum shrugged and brushed hair from my face.

"Don't worry about that for now," she replied. "Just get ready and have some breakfast."

As I showered, I remembered the tall lad bragging outside Mario's chip shop. He'd said, *maybe we sorted it for you*. Did that mean they had hurt Gurnam? But the lads were Asian, just like Gurnam. So how was it a *hate* crime? Downstairs, I kept my thoughts to myself.

"You don't *have* to visit Gurnam," Mum told me. "I'm going anyway, but if you're not up to it ..."

"No, I'm fine," I told her.

But I wasn't fine, not really. My stomach ached, and my head felt light. I had hardly touched my toast and orange juice.

"Are you sure?" Mum asked.

"Yeah," I told her.

When we reached the hospital, my stomach ache got worse. And in the lift, I wanted to puke. Hospitals reminded me of Dad. I remembered all the visits to see him after school, and the way the hospital smelled. Now I was visiting Gurnam. Part of me wanted to run away. To never see another hospital again.

At Gurnam's ward, we had to wait. The nurse gave us a warm smile and showed us to the family room.

"He has a visitor already," the nurse said.

"Oh," Mum said. "I wonder if it's Olivia?"

The nurse didn't reply. He checked his watch and left. The waiting room was shabby, with discarded magazines everywhere. The chairs were old and wobbly, and the window was dirty. We sat in silence, and I tried not to think about Dad.

Moments later, a police officer walked in. She and Mum greeted each other.

"This is PC Baker," Mum told me. "We met yesterday. I answered some questions about Gurnam."

"Did you catch his attackers?" I asked.

PC Baker shook her head. She was tall, with wide shoulders and straight blonde hair. When she smiled, it was kind and genuine.

"Not yet," PC Baker replied. "Gurnam didn't see who attacked him, but we have two witnesses who found him. Jeet, could I ask your daughter some questions?"

Mum told her that was fine.

"So, *Miss* ...?" PC Baker asked.

"Aman," I said.

"So, Aman," PC Baker replied. "Can you tell us about Mr Singh – about any threats he may have had?"

Mum gave me a small nudge and said, "The lads from the park."

I looked at Mum and gripped my seat. I couldn't bring myself to say anything.

"Come on, Aman," Mum said. "PC Baker is just trying to help Gurnam – and you."

I thought back to my first meeting with Gurnam.

"The lads tried to attack me in the park," I said at last. "Me and my dog, Milly. Gurnam saved us."

"How many lads were there?" PC Baker asked.

"Two," I replied. "One is tall, with a goatee beard. The other one is smaller and a bit spotty. He's called Sunny."

"OK," PC Baker said. "That's good. Can you tell me anything else about them – what they were wearing, if you've seen them anywhere else?"

"They're always wearing jeans and puffa jackets, and they hang around the shops near our house, too. They scare me."

"How old are they?" PC Baker asked.

I shrugged. "Older than me – maybe seventeen or eighteen?"

"Excellent," PC Baker said. "And have you ever heard them threaten Mr Singh?"

I nodded.

"Both times," I said.

"There was more than one incident?" PC Baker asked.

"Yes," I replied. "Another time they tried to mug me and my best friend in the park, but Gurnam stopped them."

"*Again?*" Mum shrieked.

I almost laughed.

"Yes, again," I said.

"How did Mr Singh stop them?" PC Baker asked.

I looked at Mum. I didn't want Gurnam to get into trouble. He had threatened the lads, but I didn't want to reveal that.

"Be honest, Aman," Mum said. "It's OK. Just tell the truth."

I gulped.

"Er …" I began. "Gurnam told them to go away. And er …"

"Go on …" Mum said.

"He just warned the lads off," I said. "He didn't attack them or anything!"

I was getting wound up. I kept thinking that Gurnam would get blamed for what happened. Like he'd only been attacked because he'd threatened the lads.

"Listen," PC Baker said, crouching in front of me. "I know you're worried, but Mr Singh isn't in any trouble, OK?"

I nodded, but I didn't believe her.

"This is a vicious hate crime," PC Baker added. "We need to stop the perpetrators before they attack …"

"But it's *not* a hate crime," I snapped. "The lads are Asian, just like Gurnam!"

PC Baker shook her head, and Mum coughed.

"Aman," Mum said. "Gurnam wasn't attacked because of his *race*. He was attacked because he's gay."

13

I stared at Mum and PC Baker.

"Gay?" I said. "Gurnam is gay?"

Mum nodded and sat beside me.

"He told me and Olivia," Mum revealed. "But he didn't want anyone else to know. I guess it doesn't matter now."

I shook my head. Why hadn't Gurnam told me? I would have understood.

"Did the lads abuse Gurnam verbally?" PC Baker asked me. "Did they say anything even a bit homophobic?"

I shook my head and thought for a moment, then I told her, "No."

And then I remembered something from the gurdwara.

"But there's something else," I said. "I saw Sunny at the Sikh temple, talking to some people. He called Gurnam nasty and said he was unnatural. That could be homophobic, couldn't it?"

PC Baker made some notes, nodding as she wrote.

"That might help," she told me.

A while later, PC Baker left the hospital. Then a nurse told us we could see Gurnam. In the corridor, a young Asian woman walked towards us. She seemed upset, so when she looked at me I smiled. She had lovely hazel eyes with light-green flecks.

They reminded me of someone, and something clicked in my head.

"Wait!" someone shouted from behind us.

It was Olivia, carrying a bunch of flowers and panting. Her face was red.

"Those bloody stairs!" Olivia said. "The lift was full, so I thought I'd get some exercise. Never again!"

Olivia, Mum and I entered the ward. Gurnam's bed was by the door, and there were nine others. All the beds were taken, but Gurnam was the only Asian patient.

"I need the loo," I said to Mum.

"OK," she replied. "We'll be with Gurnam."

I turned and hurried outside. The young Asian woman was still there, waiting for the lift. She didn't see me and moved towards the stairs.

"Excuse me!" I shouted after her.

But the woman didn't stop. I ran to the stairwell and called again.

"You came to see Gurnam!" I shouted. "Please, wait!"

The woman stopped and stared at me. Her eyes were exactly like Gurnam's and so was her frown.

"Who are you?" the woman asked as I reached her.

"My name is Aman," I replied. "Gurnam is your dad, isn't he?"

The woman gave me a sad smile.

"Is it *that* obvious?" she asked.

I nodded.

"You have the same eyes," I replied.

"How do you know my dad?" Gurnam's daughter asked.

"We're neighbours," I told her. "And he's my friend, too. Can you tell me about him?"

She frowned. She was the same height as her dad, and skinny. Her hair was dark and short, and she wore a grey jersey dress with black boots. A laptop bag hung at her side, and she smelled of sweet perfume.

"Tell you about what?" she asked. She didn't sound suspicious, just interested.

"About why he left," I said. "And why he's so sad."

She gave me another frown and told me, "You're very forward."

"I care about him," I said.

The woman sighed.

"You and me both, kid," she replied. "I'm Ria, by the way."

A bit later, Ria and I walked into the ward together. When Gurnam saw us, he couldn't hide his surprise.

"Hey!" I said, running over to hug him.

Gurnam held me tight and ruffled my hair. His eyes and cheeks were bruised, his lip was cut, and a big plaster covered his nose.

"Aman!" Gurnam said, sounding bunged up. "I see you've met my daughter."

Mum and Olivia looked confused, so I explained who Ria was. Mum stood and shook her hand.

"A pleasure to meet you, Ria," she said.

"Likewise," Ria replied.

We sat and chatted, with me perched on Gurnam's bed, until visiting time was over. We didn't say much about the attack or about Gurnam's family – we just talked about normal stuff. Afterwards, Ria was about to leave the hospital, but Mum asked her to wait.

"I don't want to hassle you," Mum said, "but we should talk about how to help your dad."

Ria looked at me and smiled.

"I see where you get it," Ria told me.

"Perhaps you could join us for dinner?" Mum said.

Ria shook her head.

"I live in London," she told us, "and I need to get back."

"Please?" I begged. "Gurnam needs us, Ria."

She thought for a moment, then shrugged.

"OK," Ria said. "But I need to make a phone call and get Dad's keys. I'll have to stay over."

Mum shook her head.

"No need," she told Ria. "We have plenty of room for you to stay."

Later that night, after Ria and Mum had talked, I knocked on the spare bedroom door. Milly was in my arms.

"I wondered how long you'd be," Ria joked. She was sitting at the desk with her laptop open.

I held Milly up and said, "I brought a puppy ..."

"Well, that's a bribe worth taking," Ria said. She grabbed Milly and gave her a cuddle. Milly had taken a shine to Ria, following her around and even sitting in her lap on the sofa after dinner.

I sat on the spare bed, and Ria closed her laptop.

"What can I tell you?" Ria asked.

I thought for a moment. During dinner, Ria had explained Gurnam's past. How he'd had to hide his sexuality from his family. How he'd married a woman just to keep his parents happy.

"Did you feel angry when he left?" I asked Ria now.

"No," she said. "I think I knew he was gay. It just seemed odd that he and Mum didn't talk and had separate bedrooms. Dad was so unhappy all the time."

"But he said that everyone judged him," I said.

Ria nodded. She wore Mum's old pyjamas and looked tired. Milly curled up on her pillow and fell asleep.

"Lots of people *did* judge him," Ria replied. "And they still do. I was the only one in our community who still wanted a relationship with him. But he vanished. And I was so worried ..."

"Where did he go?" I asked.

"Travelling – I don't know where," Ria replied. "Dad wanted to be on his own, away from everyone. When he came out as gay, it caused a huge scandal and his friends stopped talking to him. Mum acted like he'd died."

"Gurnam told me he had one really close friend," I replied.

"That would be Kully," Ria said. "Dad and Kully grew up together. But after what happened, that changed."

I thought of Lola and never speaking to her again. I just couldn't imagine it.

"So, how did you find your dad again?" I asked.

"He got in touch with me on Facebook about three months ago," Ria replied. "He'd had another episode, and his counsellor suggested it."

"An episode?" I said.

Ria nodded glumly.

"He tried to commit suicide," she told me.

I couldn't help my eyes filling up.

"I'm so sorry!" Ria said. "I shouldn't have said that. Maybe you're too young, I ..."

I shook my head.

"No," I told her. "I'm tired of people not telling me stuff."

"He means a lot to you, doesn't he?" Ria said.

"It's hard to explain," I told her. "My dad died a while back, and I've been sad ever since. It's like there's a huge hole in my life. Gurnam filled that space, sort of ..."

My words sounded weird and stupid and childish.

"Oh, Aman," Ria said. "That's ..."

But she didn't finish her sentence, so I added, "I don't know how to explain how much I want Gurnam to stick around. Dad couldn't stay – but Gurnam can, and I want him too. You're his daughter, though, so you should be the one to tell him."

"Tell him what?" Ria asked.

"That he has a reason to stay," I replied. "He needs a *reason*."

"A reason?"

"To *be*," I replied.

14

Ria stayed at ours for another night, then returned to her life in London. She promised to come back for Boxing Day, five days later. After Ria had gone, I went to help rebuild the Community Garden. The grand opening had been postponed until January, but no one wanted to wait that long. Everyone wanted it ready for Christmas. We had four days to get it done, and we were working hard.

Gurnam left hospital on 23 December – Mum took him home in our car. After lunch, Gurnam came over to the park. He looked better, but his eyes were still bruised and puffy. Mum and Olivia fussed over him until he grew annoyed.

"I'm fine!" Gurnam told them. "You're more likely to kill me than those idiots!"

Olivia grinned and called him a grumpy old git. Gurnam smiled.

"I guess that's *exactly* what I am," he replied.

Gurnam and I hadn't really spoken about Ria and his past, but I soon put that right. I waited until he took a break from the project and went for a walk, then I caught him up.

"You should have told me," I said. "About being gay."

"I didn't see the point," Gurnam replied. "It's not a big thing."

"But it *has* been a big thing," I told him. "For *you*. You've been hiding your true self for most of your life."

"It's not just that," he said. "It's leaving Ria and the others behind. I was a coward and ..."

"No," I replied. "You're not a coward. What you did was difficult for everyone, but ..."

"I'm going to turn sixty on Christmas Day," Gurnam told me. "And I feel like I've never lived."

"You have your kids," I said.

"I have Ria," he replied. "The rest of my children don't want to know me."

"But what if you tried speaking to them?" I asked. "I'm sure they'd understand that things were different when you were young ... like, you didn't have a choice."

He shook his head.

"Ria spoke to them," he revealed. "After the attack. My other kids told her I was better off dead."

I had nothing to say. I just stood and stared at Gurnam. How could they think that? He was their dad – no matter what he'd done or who he really was.

"It's OK, Aman," Gurnam said. "It's better this way. At least my life isn't fake any more. Well, what's left of it ..."

We walked the edge of the park in silence. When we got back, Olivia was handing out sausage rolls.

"Where have you two been?" she asked.

"Oh, you know," Gurnam said. "Setting the world to rights."

I told him Mum had ordered turkey and lamb for Christmas Day.

"I hope you eat lots," I added. "Mum always makes *way* too much food. You can have leftovers as a birthday present!"

"I like leftovers," Gurnam replied.

He smiled, but his eyes were distant again, as if his mind was somewhere else.

"And Ria's visiting on Boxing Day," I said. "So that'll be lovely."

"Ria rang me this morning," Gurnam told me. "She likes you. Said you were a fine young woman with a solid heart."

I grew embarrassed and had to turn away.

"She's right, too," Gurnam added. "Use that heart to help yourself, Aman. To rebuild your own life. I'm an old man, but you've got everything ahead of you."

I shook my head.

"Don't be a wally," I told him. "You're only sixty. Olivia says sixty is the new forty!"

He gave a small laugh, but his eyes stayed distant.

On Christmas Eve, I gathered together the presents Mum and I had got for Gurnam: a brand-new toolbox and tools, a torch, some work gloves and a book about Liverpool FC. I couldn't wait to see him open them all. But first we had to wrap them.

"Rule number seven in the kid and parent manual," I said to Mum. "Parent will wrap all presents and kid will watch and annoy."

Mum threw some Sellotape at me.

"Rule number one," she replied. "Cheeky kid will not get visit from Santa."

"Yeah, right," I said, rolling my eyes. "I'll get the carrots ready for Rudolph!"

We spent the whole of Christmas Eve playing games, eating nibbles and watching films on telly. Olivia came over with wine, and she and Mum got tipsy. By 11 p.m., they were both asleep in the living room. I couldn't find anything to watch on the telly, so I turned it off and went up to my room. Milly lay on my bed, snoozing too. I didn't want to disturb her, so I took my book and went back downstairs. I sat in the kitchen and read.

It was just after midnight when I heard Mum's phone vibrate in her bag on the worktop. I took her mobile out and went into the living room to give it to her. But Mum was still fast asleep, snoring gently. Then the phone vibrated again with a text message. As I read it, my whole world froze.

I'm sorry, Jeet, truly. I am just a selfish, stupid, silly old man. I've hurt everyone around me. I can't hurt anyone else. Tell Aman I'm sorry. Tell her that she isn't to blame. Tell her that I love her ...
Gurnam x

15

I only stopped to grab one thing. Then I hurried around to Gurnam's house. I started banging on the door and shouting his name, but he didn't answer.

Panicked, I went around the side. His gate was unlocked, and I ran into his garden.

The house was dark, but the garage light was on. I tried the handle of the garage door, but it was locked.

"*Gurnam!*" I shouted. My heart was racing, and my head throbbed.

The door was half wood, half frosted glass. I made out a dark human shape that had to be Gurnam. He was standing still, next to something.

"*Gurnam!*" I screamed. "*Please!*"

But he didn't move. The lights of the house next door came on, and I heard someone opening a window. I guess my screams had woken them up, but I didn't care. I reached into my pocket and took out the thing that I had grabbed from home: my letter to Dad.

"Just wait, Gurnam!" I shouted through the glass of the garage door. "Please, just listen to me. I'm begging you!"

I felt flecks of sleet begin to pepper me, and my legs shook with cold and fright. I started to read, praying that Gurnam would hear me ...

I don't want you to leave. I can't imagine my life without you, Dad. I don't want to live that life. I want my dad back. The one who picked me up when I cried, the one who read me bedtime stories. I want the Dad who smells of curry spices and beer and who taught me to ride my bike.

And I want your pain to go away. I want a magic wand to wave so that you get better. But I haven't got a magic wand, Dad. I've just got me. I can hug you and make it all better, just like you used to do. I will, Dad, I'll make it go away. I just need one more chance. Please, can I have that, Dad? Can I have that chance?

I want you to wait, if you can. I want you to hang on. Please, Dad, I need some more time. Just a little bit more time. Can you just hold on? I know I'm not very good with words, and I know that I can't change anything, but I can tell you what I want.

I want you to stay, Dad. I want you to stay. Just for a while, if nothing else. Just long enough to know that I love you. Can you try, Dad? Can you try for me? I promise I'll never ask for anything else, ever again.

I just want you to stay a little bit longer.

I could hear Mum and Olivia shouting my name. I could hear a police siren wailing somewhere close by. But none of that mattered any more. It was like I was inside a bubble, with everything else going on outside. Everything apart from Gurnam and that garage door, and what lay behind it. I can't have stood there for long, but it felt like for ever. My heart felt as if it would burst. And then I heard the lock click open ...

Gurnam stood in the doorway. His eyes were red and his cheeks hollow. Behind him was ... actually, I don't want to think about what I saw behind him. I don't want to say. Some things really are better left unsaid ...

Gurnam wiped away his tears with a meaty hand. I held out my own hand, and he took it.

"Come on," I said as Mum ran into the garden.

"But it's Christmas Day," Gurnam said. "And I've ruined it for you ..."

"Forget about Christmas," I replied. "Christmas can wait. *We'll* wait for you. Until you're better ..."

Gurnam didn't say a word. He held out a finger and wiped a tear from my face.

A police officer approached us, with a paramedic close behind. They put a blanket around Gurnam and led him away.

"Happy Birthday, Granddad," I whispered to him.

Mum put her arm around me.

"Come on," she said. "Let's get out of the cold."

EPILOGUE

On the first Saturday of March, the Christmas tree went back up. I decorated it with baubles and tinsel, and Olivia found some old chocolate Santas to hang. It wasn't quite the same as Christmas, but it was far more special. Finally, I placed Gurnam's presents under the tree and sat back to admire my work.

"Looks lovely," said Olivia. "And just in time too."

Mum's car pulled up outside. I rushed to the window, like I'd done when I was little and Dad came home.

"He's here!" I said excitedly.

"And looking so well, too," Olivia added.

After the awful events of real Christmas, Gurnam had developed pneumonia and spent a month in hospital. I had only seen him once – his choice, not mine. But I was willing to give him space, because he needed it. I missed him a lot, but he was safe and getting better. That was the most important thing.

Afterwards, Ria took him to London, to stay with her. She rang once a week, to say Gurnam was well and asking about me. But I didn't speak to him at all. I was unsure of myself and didn't want to upset him. So, I waited for him, just like I'd promised on Christmas Eve. And now he was back ...

At the door, I hesitated. I didn't know what to do. Gurnam was back to his old self. He looked healthy and happy, and his eyes held a sparkle I'd never seen before. He held out his hand.

"Hello, Aman," he said.

I smiled and took his hand.

"Hello ..."

Mum grabbed his other hand, and we led him inside.

Later, as Olivia and Mum cleared up, I got Gurnam a glass of water. He told me to sit.

"I want to thank you," he said. "You saved me..."

I didn't want to cry, but I couldn't help it. I looked away and wiped my eyes. Gurnam had saved me too – he had filled a big hole in my heart.

"I'd lost all hope until I met you and Jeet," he added. "Olivia, too. I was tired of life. I didn't believe I had anything to live for – not even Ria."

"Is that why?" I asked him. "At Christmas, when you ..."

Gurnam nodded.

"That was rock bottom," he explained. "But after you read those words, Aman ..."

He gulped and took a sip of water.

"Your words changed something inside me," he continued. "They gave me a reason ..."

"To *be* ..." I whispered.

"Yes," he replied. "Now I have something to live for."

"What's that?"

He smiled, and the warmth in his eyes made me smile too.

"You, growing up," he replied. "Ria and her partner getting married. Family ..."

"So, you're going to stay?"

"Just a little bit longer," he said. "If that's OK with you?"

I took his hand in mine and nodded.

"Welcome home, Gramps," I replied.